Fi ne

For: Vicki, Lily, Edward, and Tilly.

Rockpool Children's Books
15 North Street
Marton
Warwickshire
CV23 9RJ

First published in Great Britain by Rockpool Children's Books Ltd. 2008
Text and Illustrations copyright © Stuart Trotter / Design Concept Elaine Lonergan 2007
Stuart Trotter has asserted the moral rights
to be identified as the author and illustrator of this book.

Printed in China

rockpool
children's books

A Lift the Flap Book

Stuart Trotter & Elaine Lonergan

Fire Engine

This is Fire Engine.

**Shiny red and siren blaring,
Fighting flames, brave
and daring.**

Wash, scrub, polish, clean...

Lift
the
Flap

The call
comes in,
it's time
to go!

Lift
the
Flap

Down the street
Fire Engine flies,

Fire Engine wins the day,

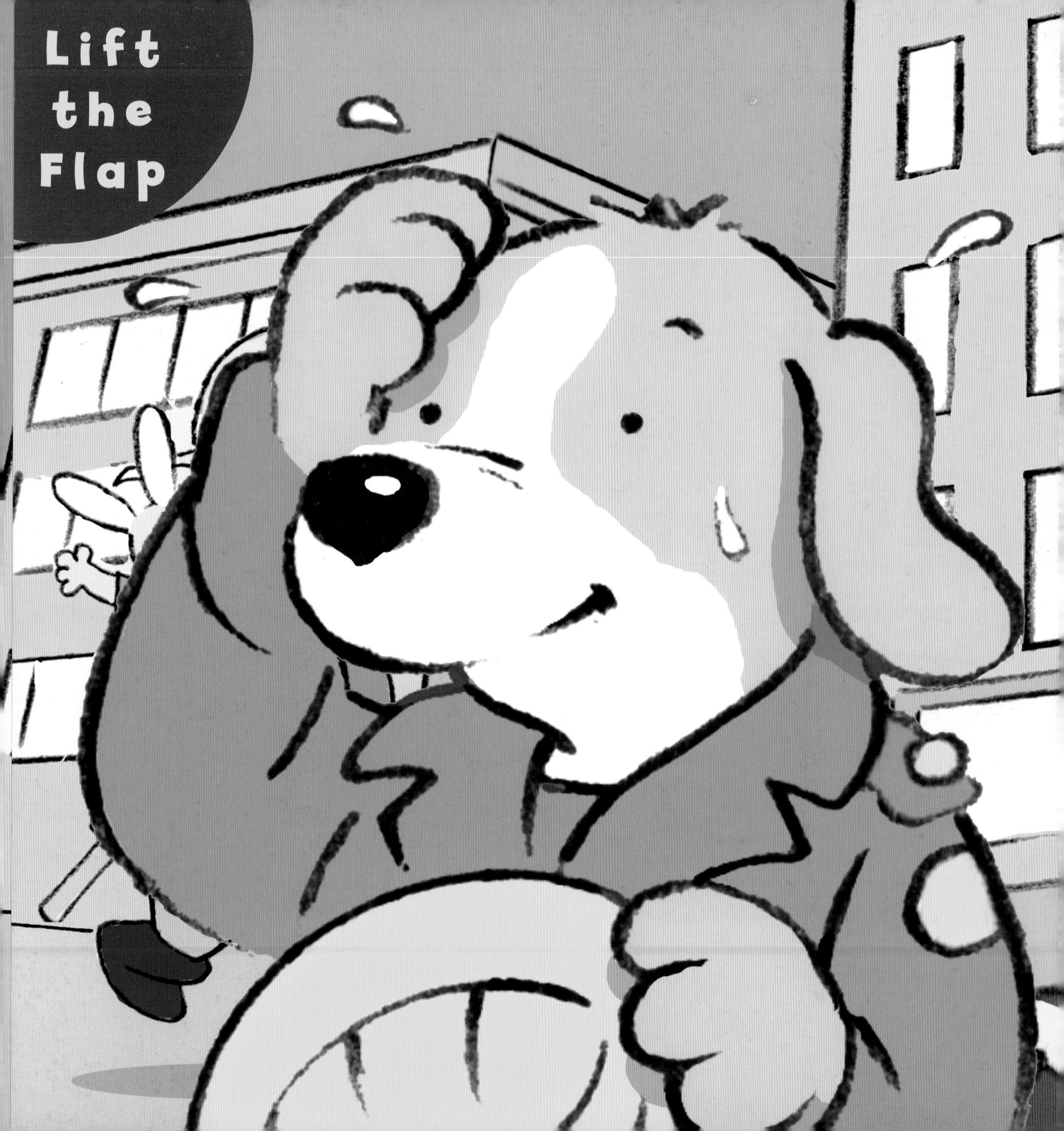
Lift
the
Flap

"Phew!" thought Fire Engine.

"What an exciting day."

He'd heard Helicopter

had been busy too....

but that's another story!

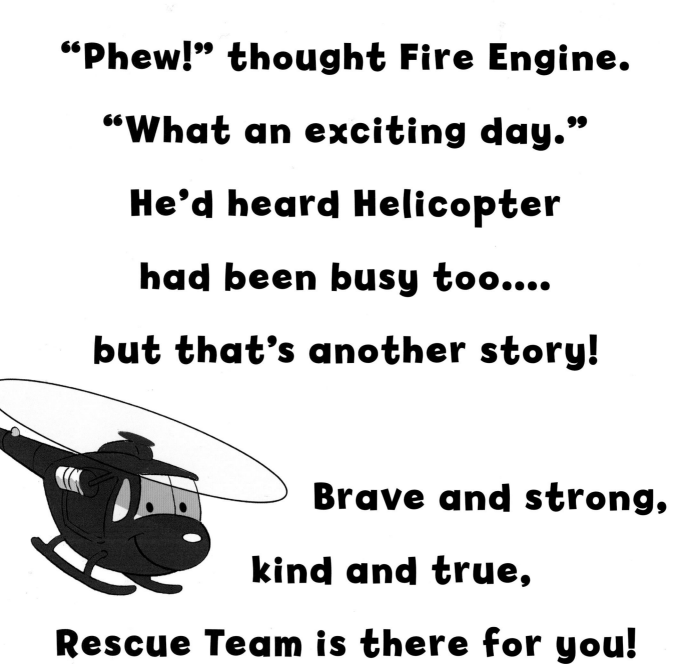

Brave and strong,

kind and true,

Rescue Team is there for you!

"Goodbye."